BRAVEMOLE

LYNNE JONELL

G. P. PUTNAM'S SONS ◆ NEW YORK

Library of Congress Cataloging-in-Publication Data
Jonell, Lynne. Bravemole / written and illustrated by Lynne Jonell.   p. cm.
Summary: A mole discovers that he is not so ordinary after all when he proves his
bravery during a dragon attack. [1. Moles (Animals)—Fiction. 2. Courage—Fiction.]
I. Title. PZ7.J675 Br 2002   [E]-dc21   2002002422
ISBN 0-399-23962-6
1 3 5 7 9 10 8 6 4 2
First Impression

For those who,
in a dark and terrifying hour,
saw what needed to be done—
and did it.

There once was a very ordinary mole.

His burrow was nothing special. There were thousands of others just like it.

His job was an ordinary one for a mole: digging, tunneling, moving a little earth from here to there.

And he loved his family in the usual kind of way—which is to say, very much.

Mole didn't mind being ordinary—not really.

But sometimes he would see Smartmoles whisking by, looking very crisp as to whiskers and very bright as to teeth, and he wondered what it would be like to be one of them, making big earthmoving plans and talk-talk-talking fast and faster because, after all, Smartmoles had a lot to say.

And sometimes he would see Bigmoles, who knew all kinds of important things, standing tall in front of other moles who asked what should be done about this, or that, and wrote down the answers; and the little ordinary mole wished that someone would ask *him* what he thought. For Mole had ideas, too.

One night, while working late, Mole even saw some Starmoles climb out of a molewagon—singing moles and dancing moles, and moles who played ball in big stadiums. "Oh," Mole thought wistfully, "they can do so many things!" And all the moles in the street cheered and cheered, and Mole cheered, too, waving his work gloves in the air. But as he was walking home, he thought what fun it would be to have a crowd cheering just for him, and he wished for a moment that he wasn't quite so ordinary.

But all this was forgotten the minute he
turned into his own front walk. Because,
after all, he had a loving molewife who
gave him a squeeze in the morning and
two at night, and a little babymole who
watched for him at the window and jumped
up and down and squealed
when Mole came through
the door.

"Daddy! Daddy! Tell me a story, Daddy!"

Mole gave his wife two squeezes and a
whisker rub, settled himself in his favorite
chair, and took Babymole on his lap.

"A story about what?"

"About dragons, Daddy. About dragons with
terrible teeth and terrible claws and fire inside!"

Mole cleared his throat and began. "Once upon
a time, long ago, there was a wicked dragon—"

Babymole bounced in his lap. "Are they real, Daddy? Dragons?"

"Oh, yes," said Mole. "Dragons are real."

"But how do you know? Did you ever see one?"

"I have never seen one. But your great-grandmoles saw one, and they
helped fight it, too."

Babymole sucked on his paw. "Will a dragon come to get me, Daddy?"

Mole shook his furry head and took a sip of his favorite tea. "No, Son.
Dragons are far away from my little babymole."

"But your bedtime is close, and your daddymole wants his supper,"
said Mole's wife cheerfully, and she swooped up Babymole in her arms
and put him to bed.

Mole woke up the next morning to a beautiful day. The trees were turning orange and red, and the sky was as blue as an open flower, with a bright yellow center. Mole ate his breakfast, kissed Babymole, and stood by the door, smiling all over his furry face as he waited for his squeeze.

"How I love you, Mole!" His wife looked up at him fondly. "You're so strong, and brave, and steady!"

Mole grew a little red about the whiskers, for he remembered all the other moles he had seen, and knew that his wife only said this because she loved him.

"No, my dear," he said, shaking his head. "I'm really a very ordinary mole, after all." But he gave her two squeezes that morning instead of one and walked out the door, whistling.

Why was it that, on this day, Mole stopped on his way to work and looked at the sky? He did not know, unless it was that beneath his furry chest, his heart was very happy. And so he said quite softly to Overmole, who hears all, "Thank you for my loving wife and little Babymole, for work I can do and for the beautiful color blue." And then, a little embarrassed, he clapped on his hat again and walked on. But he felt better for having said thanks.

And then, suddenly, there came a sound.
It was a big sound, a sound Mole had never
heard before, as if the largest tree in the forest
had fallen, hard. But the sound did not come
from the forest. It came from the place where
Mole was going, from the molehills that
had been built so tall, they were called
the Mountains.

Mole squinted. Being a mole, his eyes were not very keen, and so
at first he did not understand what he was seeing. Then
he understood but he did not believe it. And then he
believed it but he could not move, for suddenly
his knees would not hold him up. Ahead of him,
on top of the tallest molehill, was a dragon.

It was worse than any picture he had seen.
It was worse than any story he had been
told. It was worse than anything in the
world, and then moles came running,
hundreds and thousands of them. They
ran from the Mountains, where they had
worked and planned and talked, never dreaming
that a dragon was on its way, and they ran straight
toward Mole where he stood in the street.

But they were no longer Bigmoles or Smartmoles
or Starmoles or ordinary moles or any kind of mole
at all except Mole Afraid. They were all Moles Afraid
together, and Mole pressed his paws tight over his
mouth and forgot to breathe and he, too, was
Mole Afraid.

And then, high above, he saw a
second dragon soaring in. He saw its
wicked talons and its teeth as sharp as
knives. He saw the cruelty in its face
as it crashed into another tall molehill
and began to feed the fire in its belly.

Mole turned away, sick at heart. All around him were little screaming sounds and panting sounds, and choking gray smoke and terrible coughing sounds, and then up above he saw the tallest Mountain begin to crumble, with the beautiful blue sky behind it and the bright center of the sun still shining and Mole cried *"Why?"* and he would have dropped to his knees only there was no place to do it and anyway he was running so he just said it inside himself, very loud inside his head to Overmole who hears all— *"WHY?"* And Overmole did not answer.

Then somehow, he did not know how, he found himself in a sheltered place behind a rock. Mole leaned his forehead against the cool smooth stone, and thought of his little babymole and his good molewife, and he trembled. "*Why*?" he cried again, but very softly this time, and then, "*Help me.*"

Mole was silent.

And then, slowly, something stirred in his heart.

It was something strong. Something brave. Something steady.

"But what can I do?" Mole wondered. He looked at his own two paws. He looked at his feet, with their claws meant for digging. And then he knew.

"Thank you," he whispered to Overmole. Because there was a job that had to be done, and now he could do it.

Walking strongly, walking steadily, Mole pushed back the way he had come. All around him moles were still running, but here and there Mole saw that others had turned back, too. And when they saw the great Mountains crumble and fall, burying the dragons in a cloud of billowing earth and flying rock, they still trudged on. For now they were needed more than ever.

All that day and into the night Mole dug, and dug deeply.
Into the smoking rubble of the once tall Mountains his strong
paws dug, rescuing as many moles as he could find. All around
him were other moles—moles who bandaged and moles who
carried, moles who brought water and moles who put out fires,
ordinary moles and moles who were nobody special, and they
kept on working and they did not stop.

And many times Mole wanted to cry, and run away, for the work was hard and terrible. But still he kept steadily working.

And Mole knew there was danger in the work, for the gray dust choked him, and the rubble shifted beneath his feet. But still he kept bravely working.

More moles came, and brought news of other dragons that had attacked other molehills. There was talk of a distant nest where more dragons were growing. And hushed voices spoke about the strange desire of dragons to smash and destroy, and what could be done about it.

Mole listened, but he did not stop digging, though his gloves had worn through and his paws were bleeding and sore. At last, when the moon was high and his strength was gone, he staggered away from what was left of the Mountains, his heart nearly breaking in two.

His head was down as he walked, so he did not see the crowd of waiting moles. And he did not hear them until he was very close, for they were quiet, except that here and there the name of Overmole was whispered, ever so softly.

Mole looked up. Huddled close together were hundreds of moles of every kind—Smartmoles who loved to talk, Bigmoles who knew so much, Starmoles who could do so many things.

But the Smartmoles stood in silence, for they had no words for what they had seen.

And the Bigmoles bowed their heads, for there was too much they hadn't known.

And the Starmoles sat helplessly crying—for of all the wonderful things they could do, not one had been of any use.

Mole sighed, and walked faster, for he was very anxious about his loving wife and his babymole, and wanted above all else to see them safe in their own little burrow.

But then he heard a sound, soft at first but growing quickly louder, a sound he had heard before but not one he had ever expected to hear on this terrible night.

It was the sound of moles cheering, and moles clapping; moles on either side, and they were looking at *him*.

"Bravemole!" they shouted, lifting him high upon their shoulders. "Bravemole! BRAVEMOLE!"

Mole blinked, and rubbed a weary paw across his eyes, and tried to smile. But he did not feel like a Bravemole. He kept seeing the fearful face of the dragon, and the hungry fire in its belly, and the crumbling Mountains. He thought of all the little babymoles whose parents would never come home again—and somehow, being cheered by so many didn't really seem to matter anymore.

"Sir?" A Smartmole with a pencil pressed closer and got ready to write. "What do you think we should do now?"

Mole looked at her. The crowd grew quiet. And then suddenly Mole did have something to say, something important.

"Be strong," he said firmly. "Be brave. Be steady."

Mole gazed into the many different faces and saw that every eye was wet with the same bright tears. He took a deep breath, and went on.

"We are not just Smartmoles and Bigmoles and Starmoles and ordinary moles anymore. We are Moles All Together. And—we have to fight the dragons, so our babymoles won't have to."

"Bravemole! Bravemole!" they shouted again and again, waving their caps in the air. But Mole climbed quietly down and walked home, stumbling a little, because he was really very tired.

After he got home, where his frantic loving wife gave him more squeezes than he could even count, and after Mole had been fed and kissed and cried over and squeezed yet again, he settled himself in his favorite chair and took his babymole on his lap.

And Babymole, who was so little that he thought going after dragons was exciting, said, "Will *I* get to go fight the dragons, Daddy? Can I go, too?"

Mole looked at the soft furry body, and thought of the cold cruel talons of the dragon. And he held his son close, and closer.

"No," he said gently. "You will not have to fight these dragons. We grown-ups will fight them for you."

Babymole pouted and said that he wasn't afraid of any old dragons, and Mole smiled a little and shut his eyes, and listened to Babymole say his prayers. But Mole was thinking about the long hard job ahead, and how it would be done.

Of course the Bigmoles would make the decisions about fighting the dragons. And the Smartmoles would make all kinds of plans for stopping the dragons. The Starmoles would help in many different ways . . . but in the end—

". . . and deliver us from dragons," Babymole finished sleepily, nestling against his father's tired shoulder.

—In the end, there were so many more ordinary moles in the world than any other kind. They would be the ones to fight, and dig, and work, so that all the moles could build a world without dragons.

Mole rocked his babymole soft and slow, rumbling a lullaby a little off-key. His good wife came in quietly, giving his shoulders just one more squeeze, and sat beside him.

It would not be easy, Mole thought, patting his wife's furry paw with his own sore one. But Overmole helping, they would get the hard job done. Because ordinary moles were strong. And brave. And steady.

There was a city of them.
A country of them.
A whole *world* of them.

Bravemoles.